EMMA SAYS GOODBYE

EMMA SAYS GOODBYE

A Child's Guide: Bereavement

By Carolyn Nystrom
Illustrated by Annabel Large

A LION BOOK

For Sheri and her little one dancing around Jesus

Text copyright © 1990 Carolyn Nystrom
This illustrated edition © 1990 Lion Publishing

Published by
Lion Publishing
850 North Grove Avenue, Elgin, Illinois 60120, USA
ISBN 0 7459 2924 9

Editor: LaVonne Neff

First edition 1990
This paperback edition 1994

10 9 8 7 6 5 4 3 2 1

Library of Congress CIP Data applied for

Printed and bound in Singapore

"Ouch!" squeaked Emma, as she jerked her finger away from an offending pin in her square of patchwork quilt.

"Here, try this." Aunt Sue grinned and waved a thimble in Emma's direction. "It's a little hard to get used to, but it makes for happier fingers."

Emma glanced at her aunt's hands weaving even rows of eighth-inch stitches across a square of pale yellows and blues. She studied the angle of the thimble on Aunt Sue's right index finger, then slipped one on her own.

Making a quilt together had been Aunt Sue's idea, and Emma thought it was a good one. But then Emma liked most of Aunt Sue's ideas.

Pictures from their past streaked through Emma's mind. She scrambled across the sofa between them, dumping quilt scraps on the way, to give Aunt Sue a hug.

"I love you, Aunt Sue," she said. "I'm glad you came to live with us. You're my favoritest aunt."

"I love you too." Aunt Sue laughed as she took Emma in her arms. "But I don't know that 'favorite aunt' is much of a compliment. I'm also your only aunt. Your family is blessed with a bushel of uncles."

Emma picked up her quilt scraps and went back to her pictures of the past. "Do you remember the time we celebrated the last day of school? We both turned cartwheels all over the front lawn."

"The mailman—" Aunt Sue said.

They laughed together, remembering the man's surprised expression.

"And how about the time last summer when Matt was washing his new car and we leaned out of my bedroom window and dropped water balloons on him?"

"Your brother came after us both with a hose," Aunt Sue chuckled.

"I hope you stay with us forever, Aunt Sue," Emma said. "Do you have to go back to work soon?"

Aunt Sue bit her lip. "I'm not sure," she said slowly. "There's a lot I don't know right now."

Emma and her aunt sat quietly for a few minutes, their needles busy across spring pastel bits of cloth. The fabric colors echoed the apple-blossom pink, soft violet, and pale yellow of the spring outdoors whispering at their window.

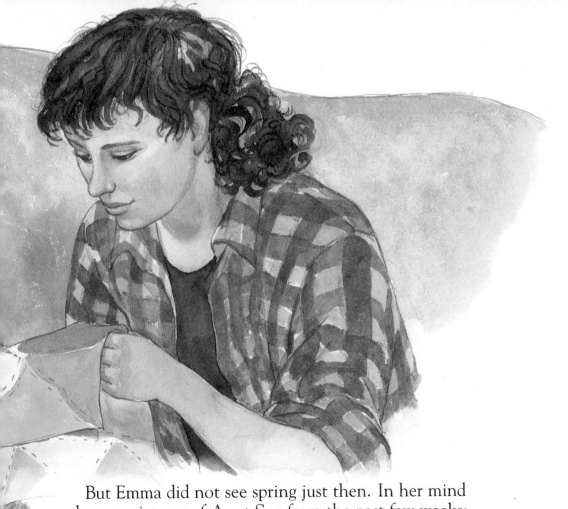

But Emma did not see spring just then. In her mind
she saw pictures of Aunt Sue from the past few weeks:
doctors' appointments, lab tests, X-ray reports, white-
uniformed nurses, surgery, hospital visits, and finally
the short trip home—to get well.

"I'll have to get a lot stronger before I can climb
telephone poles and fix wires again," Aunt Sue
sighed.

Emma bent over her quilt block of spring pastels. She fastened a pale yellow triangle to one end of a sky blue rectangle, then turned the rectangle and stitched a second yellow triangle at the other end.

She and Aunt Sue had sketched an eight-block quilt. Each of them would make four blocks—one for each season of the year. Then they would bind the eight blocks together with colored patchwork squares from all the seasons. Finally, once the batting and lining were in place, they would take tiny, tiny stitches around the edge of each quilt piece to make it stand out from the rest.

Aunt Sue broke the silence. "What does this square make you think of?" she asked.

Emma squeezed her lips together, turned her square from one side to the other and squinted at it.

"I'm not sure," she said. "From this side, it looks like the shovel Mom used yesterday to dig holes for her new rose bushes— except it has a point on the other end instead of a handle. But when I turn it this way, it looks like two oars for a boat."

"A boat in a rushing spring creek," Aunt Sue said. "I'd like to jump in right now."

"What does your square make you think of?" Emma returned the question.

"I was thinking of the bar and two triangles as an arrow that shoots two ways," Aunt Sue said thoughtfully. "One end points to heaven, and the other points to earth."

Emma wondered why Aunt Sue had her mind on heaven just then, but she couldn't think of a good way to ask. So she put a worried pucker on her forehead instead.

Summer got a hard start at Emma's house. Its long hot days found Aunt Sue going every morning to the hospital for medicine. Her doctor hoped this "chemotherapy" would kill the cancer cells in her body. But he warned her that the medicine would make her feel sick because it would kill good body cells too.

Aunt Sue lay on the sofa every afternoon. Sometimes Emma brushed her aunt's hair. Sometimes they watched TV together. Sometimes they read. And sometimes Emma got tired of being with a sick person all the time—even Aunt Sue. So she went away and played with her friends.

Each week Aunt Sue seemed to take less space as her body got thinner and thinner. Often she felt sick to her stomach most of the day. By evening she could keep some soft food down, but in the morning it was time to return to the hospital for more medicine. Then the sick feeling would start all over again.

One frightening day, Aunt Sue's curly brown hair fell out in great clumps across the sofa pillows. Emma saw tears in her aunt's eyes as she swept the curls into the trash basket. Then Aunt Sue walked slowly to her room and came back with a wig that she and Emma's mom had bought early in the summer—just in case.

On evenings when Aunt Sue did not feel well
enough to eat at the table, Emma's family brought
their food on trays to eat with her. Before their meal,
they all paused to thank God for their food, as they
always did. The one who said grace also asked God to
help Aunt Sue get well.

At the end of the meal, if Aunt Sue felt especially
bad, they all held hands in a circle with her and sang.
Sometimes they sang "Praise God from Whom All
Blessings Flow." And sometimes, instead of singing,
Mom or Dad would read a Psalm from the Bible.

It was a long seven weeks, but the chemotherapy
did its work. Tests showed that Aunt Sue's blood was
getting back to normal. Aunt Sue began to eat and
laugh again. Even her hair grew back in fuzzy tufts like
a boy's crew cut.

One bright blue August day Aunt Sue and Emma
rented a canoe and paddled down a stream overhung
by swamp willows. Aunt Sue sat in front, and Emma
steered with the back oar.

"Stroke, stroke!" Aunt Sue sang out as they dipped
their oars in unison first to one side and then the
other. Emma watched a willow branch brush Aunt
Sue's thin white shoulder and remembered last
summer when Aunt Sue glowed with the dark tan and
strong muscles of a telephone line worker.

What about next summer? Emma wondered. Will
Aunt Sue be healthy and strong and working again? Or
will she . . ?

No, of course not, Emma's thoughts objected. The
doctor is working hard. And God won't let her die . . .
not if we keep asking him to make her well.

Just then a screech from the front of the canoe brought Emma back to the present.

"Hey, give that back!" Aunt Sue shouted to a low-hanging birch.

Her wig waved defiantly from a sturdy twig as the summer breeze ruffled her short tufts of hair and the current carried them downstream.

Emma and her aunt turned the canoe around. Twice they nearly got stuck in the bank, and once Emma jumped into the shallow water to keep the canoe from overturning. Finally they made it back to the birch tree.

Aunt Sue grabbed the wig from the branch, shook a scolding finger at the tree, and jammed the wig on her head—sideways, just to be silly.

Emma laughed until her sides hurt.

That evening, lightning crackled at their living
room windows while thunder crashed overhead.
Emma opened the curtains so that she and Aunt Sue
could watch as jagged streaks of lightning sawed
through boiling clouds. Emma rested her head on her
aunt's shoulder and felt safe. The violence outside
contrasted with the warm dry quiet of the living
room. Gradually the intervals between flash and
rumble grew longer. Then torrents of rain lashed
against the window, blotting out their view of the sky.

Aunt Sue picked up quilt scraps as Emma turned on a lamp. This time they were stitching zigzag strips of poppy red on brilliant summer sky blue. Apple-green triangles braced the corners.

Emma traced the red edges with her needle. "It looks like lightning," she said. "Except it's the wrong color. I wonder if lightning is ever red."

"I don't think so," answered her aunt. "Maybe with the right kind of clouds or haze. . ." she continued doubtfully. "But it reminds me of lightning too."

They listened to the pounding rain.

"Lightning really does cut through the sky, doesn't it," Emma said, remembering science class. "I think that's what makes the thunder—the air slamming back together after the lightning slices it apart."

"Something like that," murmured Aunt Sue. "This zigzag lightning piece reminds me of a gap that slices like lightning between people."

"Like when they get mad at each other and won't talk?" Emma asked.

"Yes," Aunt Sue replied. "Or when they move far away from each other and can't be together anymore."

Emma and her aunt stitched silently for a moment. "Or when they die," Emma murmured softly.

But Aunt Sue didn't hear.

As summer with all its energy waned into fall, Emma saw her aunt's energy also lag. First she saw small changes like the dark circles under her eyes in the mornings. Her footsteps on the wood floors sounded slow and shuffling, and she seemed to eat even less.

Emma returned to school, Matt went off to college—and Aunt Sue went back to the hospital. The cancer had returned. While Emma worked at fractions and long division, Aunt Sue had X-rays and blood tests.

Soon Aunt Sue was back home. Once again she spent most of her day on the living room sofa, and once again she traveled every day to the hospital—this time for radiation therapy. Aunt Sue explained that machines sent X-rays into her body to try to burn up the cancer cells. The X-rays also burned her skin and made it red and sore. The X-rays seemed to burn up her energy too; she felt more tired than ever.

Emma's mom quit her job so that she could be home with Aunt Sue all the time.

One crisp October day, Emma scuffed home from school through gold and crimson leaves layered ankle deep on the sidewalk. Everything felt brittle—the crunch of leaves swishing by her legs, the cool bite in the steel blue air, the snap in the taut maroon skin of the apple left from lunch in her jacket pocket.

As she came near the sidewalk to her house, Emma slowed her steps. She looked up at the porch sagging slightly under the weight of its roof, and she felt her shoulders sag. Last spring she would have leaped up the porch steps two at a time, but today she stopped, shuffled the leaves on the sidewalk with her feet, pulled out the apple and began a private afternoon snack.

Finally, apple core in hand, she entered the front door. Her whole house smelled sick, as she knew it would. Even Mom's homemade vegetable soup simmering on the stove couldn't drive the smell away.

Emma dumped her apple core in the garbage, then swept from the counter half-empty baby-food jars and soggy paper cups of ice water: Aunt Sue's lunch.

"How is she today?" she asked her mother, who had just appeared in the doorway.

"About the same," came the wooden reply.

"When is she going to get better?" Emma sighed. "I'm tired of Aunt Sue being sick."

Mom didn't answer.

Emma saw that her mother's tired gray eyes didn't quite meet hers. Instead they seemed to look at a point somewhere behind her left shoulder.

Emma felt her mouth go dry. "She's not going to get well, is she, Mom?" A shudder rocked her whole body. "Aunt Sue is going to die!"

Mom held her close and stroked her hair until her shaking stopped.

"Does she know?" Emma whispered.

Mom nodded.

"Is it all right if I talk to her about it?"

"I think that would be good for both of you," Mom agreed.

That evening Emma and her aunt stitched once
again on their quilt. This time they were not in the
living room. Aunt Sue sat propped up in her bed with
pillows all around so that nothing hard would touch
her sensitive skin. Mom had fastened bags onto the
side of the bed to hold the things Aunt Sue needed.
Her quilt scraps lay in a basket on the floor. The
curtains were open, even though it was nearly dark,
because Aunt Sue liked to watch the last hint of
twilight.

They stitched quietly for a while, working on the
autumn shades of gold and crimson and olive green.
In the middle of their square was a large, brown,
somewhat oval shape. Emma, in a whimsical moment,
had made the pattern by tracing around one of her

father's shoes. Aunt Sue had liked its shape, and so they had designed it into their autumn quilt square.

Emma felt a lump in her throat getting bigger and bigger until she could hardly swallow at all.

Finally she said, "Aunt Sue, you're not getting better are you?"

"No, I'm not."

"And you aren't ever going to get well and go back to work?"

"No."

"Aunt Sue, I love you." Emma put her arms around her aunt's thin shoulders and felt her short bristly hair against her face.

"Last spring, I thought you'd come here to live with us," she said. "But you didn't. You came here to die."

"How could God let you die?" Emma asked. "We've asked him every day to make you better."

Aunt Sue was quiet for a moment. Then she spoke slowly. "I know that God hears our prayers. And I know that he loves us. But he doesn't always give us what we ask—even when it is as important as life. I don't know why."

Emma felt anger creep up the back of her neck: anger at her parents for bringing Aunt Sue into her quiet healthy home, anger at Aunt Sue for being sick, anger at the doctors for not making her well, and even anger at God—a God who was supposed to love them, but who was going to let Aunt Sue die anyway.

Aunt Sue seemed to mirror her thoughts.

"Sometimes I look at this skinny sick body of mine, and I get mad," she said. "This isn't the me I want to be!" She slapped her thin leg. "I don't know why God is letting this happen to me, but I know he's promised the people who love him that he'll never leave them alone. I think of him when I look at that big footprint on our quilt. No matter what happens, God keeps right on walking with me. So even when I die, I won't die alone."

Autumn rustled into winter. Matt came home from college for Christmas. Emma watched his eyes widen when he saw Aunt Sue's thin sick frame propped up in a hospital bed in her room. He kissed Aunt Sue lightly on the cheek, touched her cropped hair, and then whirled out, closing the door to his own room. Usually when Matt was home the house was full of music and friends. But this year, Matt went away a lot. And when he played music, it was soft guitar late at night alone in his room. Emma missed him.

Christmas Day dawned gray and damp-cold. By ten o'clock lacy flakes the size of quarters drifted from the sky, etching the black trees with white. A fire crackled through apple logs in the fireplace. On the stereo a choir sang Handel's *Messiah* while the family opened gifts. Everything seemed slower and quieter this year. For one thing, Aunt Sue wasn't scrambling around the room trying to see all the presents at once. Instead, she sat, small and frail, propped in a wheelchair. But she had done her shopping. Aunt Sue gave Emma a bright green sweater she'd picked out in a catalog.

Emma had thought a long time about what to give Aunt Sue. (What do you give a person who is dying?) Finally she chose a large picture book of a story Aunt

Sue had read to her when she was little. Aunt Sue's smile showed that she remembered. They would read it again.

"Hallelujah!" rang out trumpets, strings and voices on the stereo.

"The kingdom of this world is become the kingdom of our Lord, and of his Christ: and he shall reign for ever and ever."

"What this party needs is a little dancing," said Aunt Sue. "And that is just the kind of music to dance to. I'm not quite up to it at the moment, but give me some time." She wiggled expectantly in her wheelchair. "One of these days I'm going to be as alive as a new colt, and I'm going to dance around Jesus."

It was hard not to smile, Aunt Sue seemed so eager. Emma sprang up. "Why not get started right now?" she

said. She swung her new green sweater across her
shoulders and whirled around the living room,
stooping every now and then to touch Aunt Sue, who
clapped her hands in time to the music.

The trumpets soared higher and higher as the
chorus sang the final words—"King of Kings, and Lord
of Lords, Hallelujah!"

January turned bitter cold. Long blue shadows of bare trees crept across the snow. A hospice worker visited each day to help with Aunt Sue's medicines and bath. An oxygen tank stood near the bed to ease her breathing when she needed it. Emma came each day after school to her aunt's room. Each day Aunt Sue seemed weaker.

The quilt came out only once in January. One pale afternoon, they pieced the winter block—a large white circle edged with grays and black. Aunt Sue leaned on one bony elbow and tried to stitch with the other hand, but the position made breathing hard. She stopped sewing for a moment to rest.

"That circle is like life, Emma," she said. "You put your needle in at one point and you pick it up somewhere else. It never ends."

Emma dropped her own square and met her aunt's eyes. "Like when Jesus died," Emma said, "he came back to life?"

"Yes, and we will too," her aunt said. "People who love Jesus move from life here to life with him. Death doesn't end life. Life just begins again in heaven."

Emma nodded. She felt her chin trembling. "But I'll miss you terribly here," she cried.

"I know," her aunt replied.

Aunt Sue handed over her block. "Here. You'll have to finish this."

Then she leaned back on her pillows and began to breathe more easily.

The next morning, Emma heard hushed voices,
even before she opened her eyes. She stumbled into
her aunt's room. Mom and Dad were both there. The
oxygen machine was running. Aunt Sue's breathing
was fast and shallow. She stirred restlessly, but seemed
asleep.

Dad stayed home from work that day, and Emma
stayed home from school. Mom called Matt at
college. Mom and Dad took turns sitting in Aunt
Sue's room. They held her thin hand and talked to
her. Sometimes she seemed to squeeze a hand in
return, but she didn't open her eyes.

By late afternoon Aunt Sue's breathing got slower and slower. Emma and her parents stood together near the bed. Dad opened his Bible and began to read.

"For I am certain that nothing can separate us from God's love: neither death nor life . . . There is nothing in all creation that will ever be able to separate us from the love of God which is ours through Christ Jesus our Lord."

While Dad was reading, Matt slipped into the room, guitar in hand. Softly he began to sing, "Jesus Loves Me." During the song, Emma saw her aunt search for one last breath—then stop. Her family held each other and cried.

Months later, spring sun warmed Emma's back as she spread her newly finished quilt on the shaded grass to dry. Mom had helped with batting and lining and border. But Emma had quilt-stitched around the edges of each piece herself. Her stitches got smaller and more regular as she went along. By the end, she had trouble telling which pieces were Aunt Sue's and which were her own. The colors of the seasons, each with its own memories, blended into the background of green grass.

The cold of January blurred into the past. A house full of relatives, neighbors, and friends. A refrigerator packed with food brought by people who wanted to help. A casket with a spray of flowers on top and Aunt Sue inside looking asleep in her long- sleeved blue silk dress. Friends standing in front of the casket and crying. A funeral at church full of music and words from the Bible about living forever in heaven with Jesus, where people play and sing and dance and work, and no one ever, ever cries.

A gaping hole in snow-edged cemetery ground. Aunt Sue's casket lowered down inside and covered with cold chunks of black earth. The words of Jesus, read aloud: "I am the resurrection and the life. He who believes in me will live, even though he dies."

Emma watched the warm sun filter through green leaves toward her quilt, the quilt she and Aunt Sue had made in their year together. And somehow the light-filtered air of spring made it easy to believe that somewhere in greener grass, under bluer skies and lusher trees, Aunt Sue was tall and tan and strong—and dancing around Jesus.